P9-DHM-907

© 2007 Disney Enterprises, Inc./Pixar

All rights reserved.
Published by Scholastic Inc., 90 Old Sherman Turnpike, Danbury, Connecticut 06816.

No part of this publication may be reproduced in whole or in part, or stored in a retrieval
system, or transmitted in any form or by any means, electronic, mechanical, photocopying,
recording, or otherwise, without written permission of the copyright holder.

SCHOLASTIC and associated logos are trademarks and/or registered
trademarks of Scholastic Inc.

For information regarding permission, write to:
Disney Licensed Publishing, 114 Fifth Avenue, New York, New York 10011.

978-0-439-02415-0
0-439-02415-3

Printed in the U.S.A.
First printing, May 2007

DISNEY·PIXAR

RATATOUILLE
(rat·a·too·ee)

SCHOLASTIC INC.

New York   Toronto   London   Auckland   Sydney
Mexico City   New Delhi   Hong Kong   Buenos Aires

6

Deep in the French countryside, a colony of rats sifted through a compost heap for food. It was a dirty job, but Remy had to sniff all the scraps of bread, vegetables, and who knows what else to make sure they were safe to eat. His brother, Emile, was always impressed by Remy's sense of taste and smell.

Secretly, Remy had a bigger dream than rummaging through trash. He wanted to be a great chef, like his idol Auguste Gusteau. Remy had even read Gusteau's book *Anyone Can Cook!*

Both the cookbook and the compost heap belonged to an old woman named Mabel. Mabel's attic was home to the whole rat colony, although Mabel had no idea the rats lived upstairs.

One day, as Remy sneaked into her kitchen to look for a spice, he heard Gusteau's name. Remy learned that the great chef had died from a broken heart after his restaurant lost its five-star rating.

Remy was so shocked by the news about
Gusteau that he didn't notice Mabel waking up.
He and Emile scrambled to escape as Mabel
chased them. In the chaos, the ceiling cracked
and the entire rat colony fell to the floor.

"Sound the alarm! Evacuate!" cried out
Remy's father, Django.

As the other rats headed out the door, Remy
went back into the kitchen for the cookbook.
He couldn't leave it behind!

Unfortunately, Remy was left behind! All the other rats made it to the evacuation boats that were floating in the creek.

Separated from his family, the little rat tried to use the cookbook as a raft, but was swept away, taking a wild ride down into the sewer pipes. When he finally came to a stop, he was all alone, hungry, and sad.

Soon after, Remy began to dry out his precious cookbook pages. Magically, Gusteau seemed to come to life on the page. Or was it Remy's imagination? "If you arc hungry, go up and look around," said Gusteau. "If you focus on what you've left behind, you will never be able to see what lies ahead."

GUSTEAU'S

And that's exactly what
Remy did. He climbed up
and up until he saw . . .

"Paris?" Remy said breathlessly. "All this time I've been underneath Paris? Wow! It's beautiful!"

Remy looked to his left. His jaw dropped. He saw the sign for Gusteau's restaurant.

"*Your* restaurant?" Remy said to Gusteau. "You've led me to your restaurant!"

For Remy, this was a dream come true.

Remy perched atop the restaurant's skylight, looking down into the kitchen. At that moment an awkward-looking young man named Linguini arrived with a letter for Skinner, the ill-tempered chef in charge of the kitchen. Linguini's mother had been a good friend of Gusteau's. She wanted her son to have a job at the restaurant.

Skinner had no choice. He hired Linguini as the garbage boy.

A little while later, Linguini accidentally spilled a pot
of soup. Remy watched in horror as Linguini secretly added
water and ingredients to the pot in an attempt to fix the soup.

Just then, Remy fell down from the skylight and landed in the busy kitchen crowded with chefs! He scrambled to escape through an open window.

Remy ran by the big pot of soup—
then stopped short. It smelled horrible!
Encouraged by Gusteau, Remy thought this
was his chance. Remy knew *he* could fix
the soup! He jumped onto the stovetop and
started tossing carefully picked ingredients
into the pot.

As Remy worked he suddenly realized that a huge face was staring at him. It was Linguini. But Skinner was right behind him! Linguini quickly hid Remy under a colander.

Skinner shouted at Linguini. "How dare you cook in my kitchen!" He fired Linguini on the spot.

Before anyone knew it, the questionable bowl of soup was on its way to the dining room where an important restaurant critic sat waiting to eat.

Everyone in the kitchen was nervous as to what the critic thought about the soup. Word came back: the soup was delicious! The critic loved it!

Skinner couldn't believe it, so he tasted the soup himself. It tasted incredible!

"Um . . . am I still fired?" asked Linguini.

Reluctantly, Skinner gave Linguini a second chance. He assigned Colette, one of the cooks, to teach Linguini.

In the commotion, Remy darted towards the window. But Skinner spotted Remy.

After ordering Linguini to catch the rat in a jar, Skinner demanded, "Take it away from here, far away. Dispose of it. Go!"

Linguini didn't have the heart to throw Remy in the river. Instead, the young man started talking to the little rat. When Remy nodded, Linguini realized that Remy understood him. Linguini made a deal with his new rat friend: Linguini would let Remy out of the jar if the rat promised to help Linguini cook.

But as soon as Linguini opened the jar, Remy ran for his life. Then he stopped. Remy felt guilty, and turned back. He felt bad for Linguini, but he also realized that this could be *his* big chance to cook in a gourmet kitchen!

Back inside the restaurant, Linguini hid Remy in his shirt as Remy tried to help the young chef with his cooking. But Remy kept tickling and biting Linguini to guide him along. Ouch! It didn't work very well.

Finally Linguini hid the rat under his chef's hat. In the bustling kitchen, the pair was about to collide with the waiter, so Remy tugged Linguini's hair. Linguini jerked backwards like a puppet, just ducking under the waiter's tray. The young man was amazed. Could this be their new system?

Linguini and Remy went home to practise cooking. Remy guided Linguini by tugging his hair. Before long, Linguini was chopping, mixing, and pouring—all the while blindfolded!

Linguini returned to Gusteau's and re-created the soup easily, with Remy's help. Before long, Linguini was doing very well as the new cook. In the meantime, Skinner finally read the letter from Linguini's mother. In it, she said that Auguste Gusteau was Linguini's father. Nobody knew, not even Linguini—or Gusteau!

Skinner was horrified. He had thought the restaurant would be his.

Skinner's lawyer reminded the chef what was in Gusteau's will. The will said Skinner would inherit the restaurant—but only if Gusteau had no heirs. Now Linguini was the rightful owner. Skinner had to do something to make sure Linguini never found out.

One night, as Remy was relaxing in the alley behind the restaurant, enjoying a cooking success, Emile appeared!

Emile led his long-lost brother to the rat colony's new home. Overjoyed, they held a party in honor of Remy's homecoming. Music and dance filled the sewer.

Soon Remy had to leave. He said that he had a job and a place to live—with humans. Remy's father scowled and tried to convince his son that humans were dangerous. He took Remy to an exterminator's shop that specialized in getting rid of rats. Against his father's wishes, Remy headed back to the restaurant.

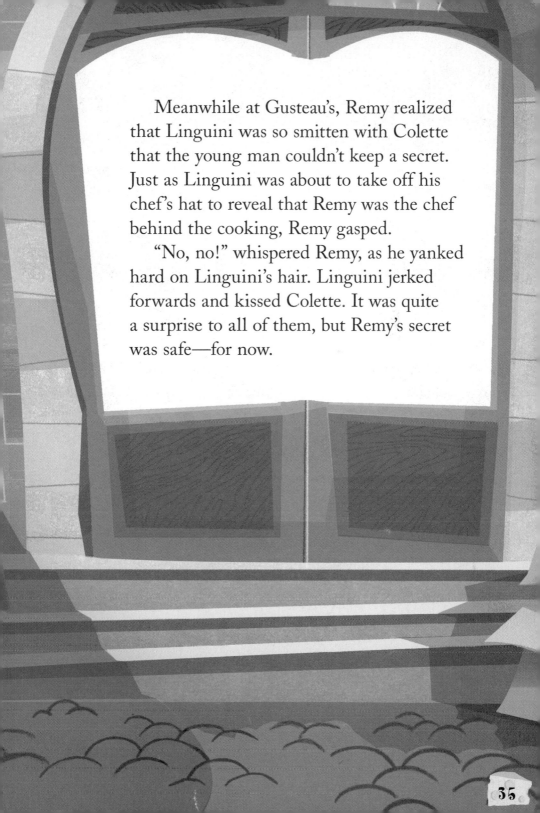

Meanwhile at Gusteau's, Remy realized that Linguini was so smitten with Colette that the young man couldn't keep a secret. Just as Linguini was about to take off his chef's hat to reveal that Remy was the chef behind the cooking, Remy gasped.

"No, no!" whispered Remy, as he yanked hard on Linguini's hair. Linguini jerked forwards and kissed Colette. It was quite a surprise to all of them, but Remy's secret was safe—for now.

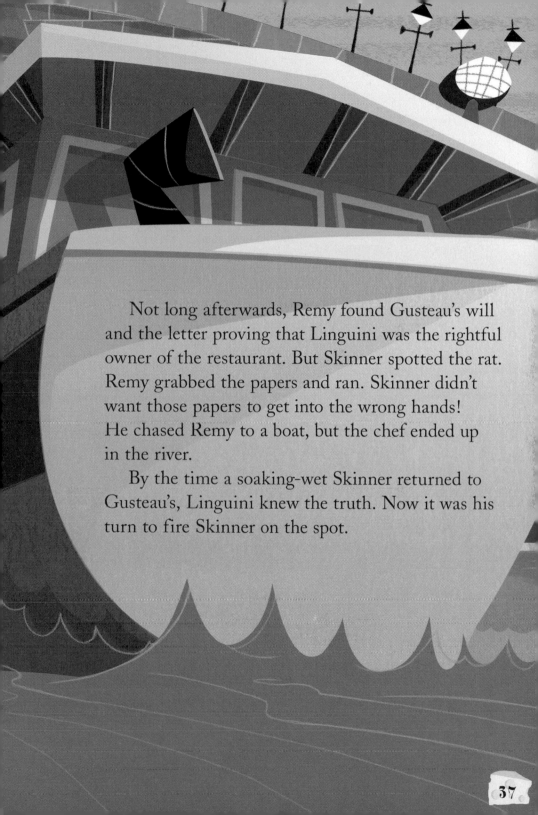

Not long afterwards, Remy found Gusteau's will
and the letter proving that Linguini was the rightful
owner of the restaurant. But Skinner spotted the rat.
Remy grabbed the papers and ran. Skinner didn't
want those papers to get into the wrong hands!
He chased Remy to a boat, but the chef ended up
in the river.

By the time a soaking-wet Skinner returned to
Gusteau's, Linguini knew the truth. Now it was his
turn to fire Skinner on the spot.

Over the next few weeks, the restaurant became extremely popular. But Linguini became arrogant and didn't think he needed Remy's help any longer.

One night, the famous critic Anton Ego—the same person who had ruined Gusteau's five-star rating—arrived and warned: "I will return tomorrow night with high expectations."

After Ego's announcement, Colette angrily
dragged Linguini back into the kitchen, trying to get him
to concentrate. Remy was also furious at Linguini's careless
behavior and pulled his hair hard.

Linguini snapped. He took Remy out to the alley and
yelled, "You take a break, Little Chef. I'm not your puppet!"

Remy was so angry that he brought the entire rat colony to the walk-in refrigerator and told his friends to take what they wanted.

That's when Linguini returned to apologize.

"You're stealing from me?" Linguini angrily asked Remy. "I thought you were my friend. Get out and don't come back!" Remy left the kitchen.

The next day Remy went back because he felt horrible and knew Linguini needed his help.

"Rat!" shrieked all the chefs when Remy walked through the door.

"Don't touch him!" shouted Linguini. "The truth is, I have no talent at all. But this rat—he's the real cook."

All the cooks walked out—even Colette. Only Remy and Linguini were left to cook for Ego.

Django stepped out from the shadows. "I was wrong about you. About him," Django told Remy, referring to how Linguini stood up for the little rat. "I'm proud of you."

Django whistled, and the rats filled the kitchen. "We're not cooks, but you tell us what to do, and we'll get it done." All the while, the health inspector watched through the door.

Just then, Colette returned and agreed to help cook the dish Remy had chosen: ratatouille. After sampling the meal, Ego asked to meet the chef. Linguini introduced Remy. Without a word, Ego walked out to pen his review.

The next morning, Ego gave the restaurant a glowing critique! Unfortunately, the health inspector also closed Gusteau's—due to rats.

But soon, a new little bistro opened: La Ratatouille, which became famous for its delicious food. Ego was an investor, Linguini was the waiter, and Colette cooked—along with Remy. The little rat's dream had come true. He was a chef at last.

EYE SPY

Take a mouth-watering journey back through the story and try to find these pictures.